'Iwalani's Tree

written by
Constance Hale

illustrated by
Kathleen Peterson

BeachHouse

I like to lean on a low branch
of a tree
that stands way way down the beach,
toward Ka'ena,
just on the spot
where the land becomes sand.

Some people call it a paina,
some call it an ironwood.
It has fuzzy brown bark,
a trunk strong and good,
and long willowy needles
that whisper in the wind.

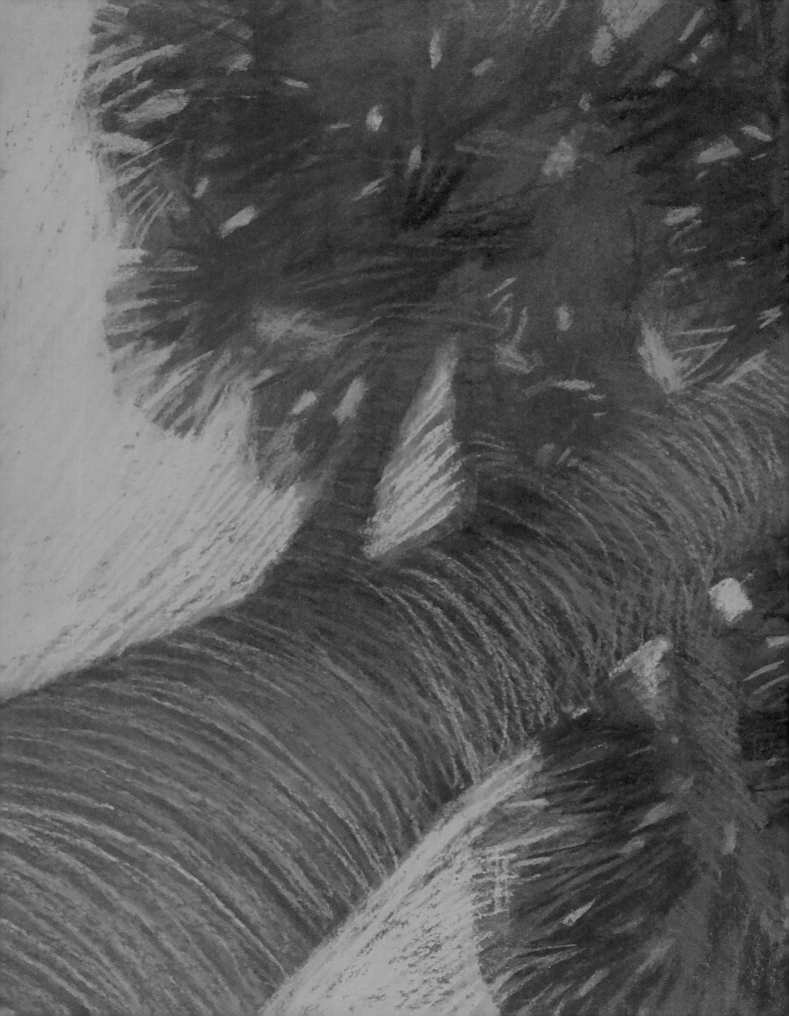

Sometimes, when a light breeze,
he makani aheahe,
tickles her needles,
the tree whispers soft sounds
like those you hear
when you hold a shell to your ear.

Sounds of the sea and the sand
and the waves and the wind:
*whaaaaaah shhhhh paaaaah
whooooshh aaaaaaaaahhhh.*

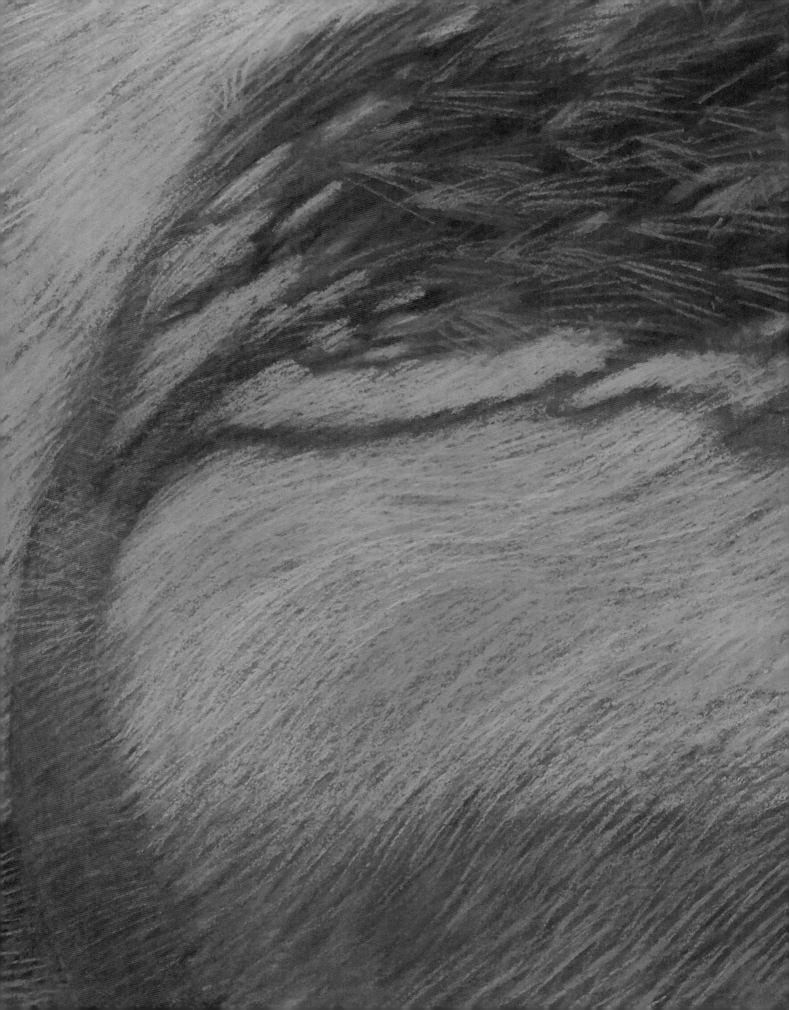

And sometimes, when a brisk wind,
he makani Mālua,
makes her branches bend and bellow,
the tree yowls scary sounds
like those you hear in a deep dark rainforest.

Sounds of the mongoose and the pueo,
of hawks and puaʻa:
    grrrrrr neckle ummmmmmmmbrrrrr.

I like to walk toward Ka'ena,
to the tree's spot,
when the house is too hot
or my brother is bothering me
or the neighbors are making much
too much noise.

My tree never says things that people say, like
      "Don't just sit there like a bump on a log!"
            or
      "Eh, you goin' moemoe?"
            or
      "Stop daydreaming!"

She likes it when I sit and dream,
and sometimes she does say things to me,
but only when the wind blows:
      whaaaaaah shhhhh paaaaah
      whooooshh aaaaaaaaahhhh
         and
      grrrrrr neckle ummmmmmmbrrrrr.

The tree's branches bend and lean
over the beach.
Her shadow makes a pool of cool,
and her fallen needles float out
like Mr. Tanaka's great green net.

I sit in the shade
and fish for my favorite treasures:
        crunchy pine cones
        blue beach glass
        skeletons of sea urchins
        and shells of every shape.

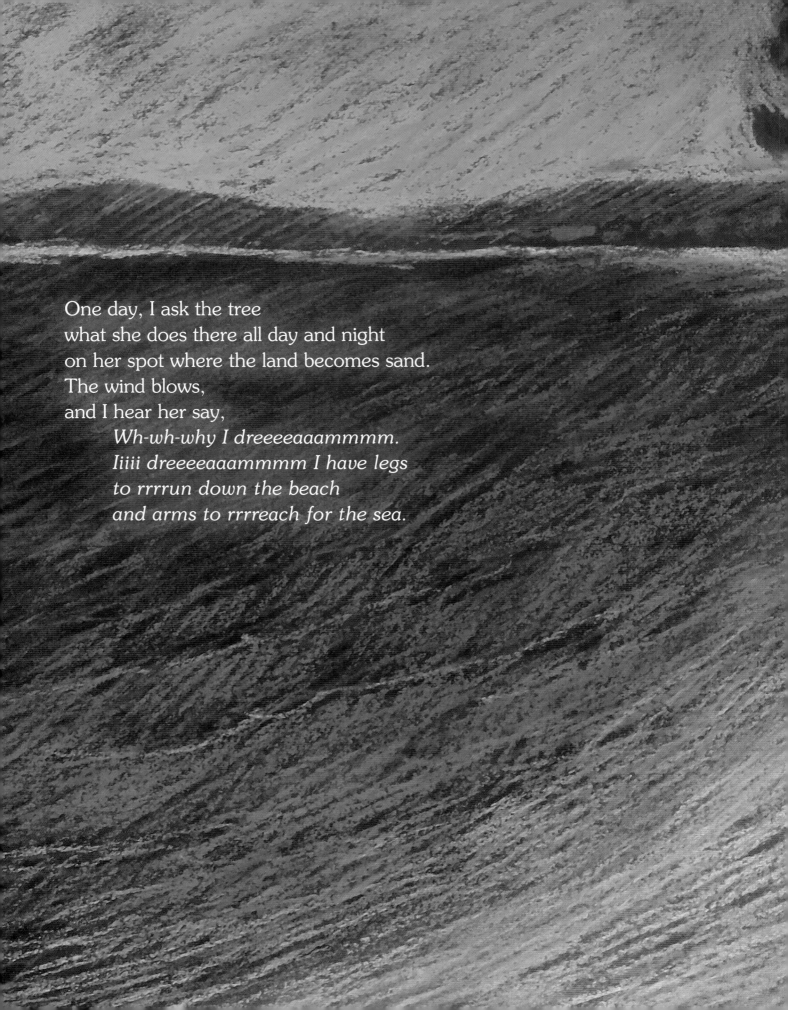

One day, I ask the tree
what she does there all day and night
on her spot where the land becomes sand.
The wind blows,
and I hear her say,
> Wh-wh-why I dreeeeaaammmm.
> Iiiii dreeeeaaammmm I have legs
> to rrrrun down the beach
> and arms to rrrreach for the sea.

Isn't that silly?
Who ever heard
of a tree with arms and legs??!!

But could it be?

One night, when I am home
and in my bed,
a big storm
comes in from the sea.

Huge white waves smash onto the sand.
A howling wind tears the leaves off trees.
Lightning cracks the sky open like a coconut.

In the morning, I see that the storm
sent palm fronds crashing to the ground
and stole the tin roof
off of Mrs. DaSilva's chicken coop.

Did the storm also take my tree
and carry her off to sea?
I race way way down the beach,
toward Ka'ena.

My tree still stands
just on the spot
where the land becomes sand.
But something has changed.

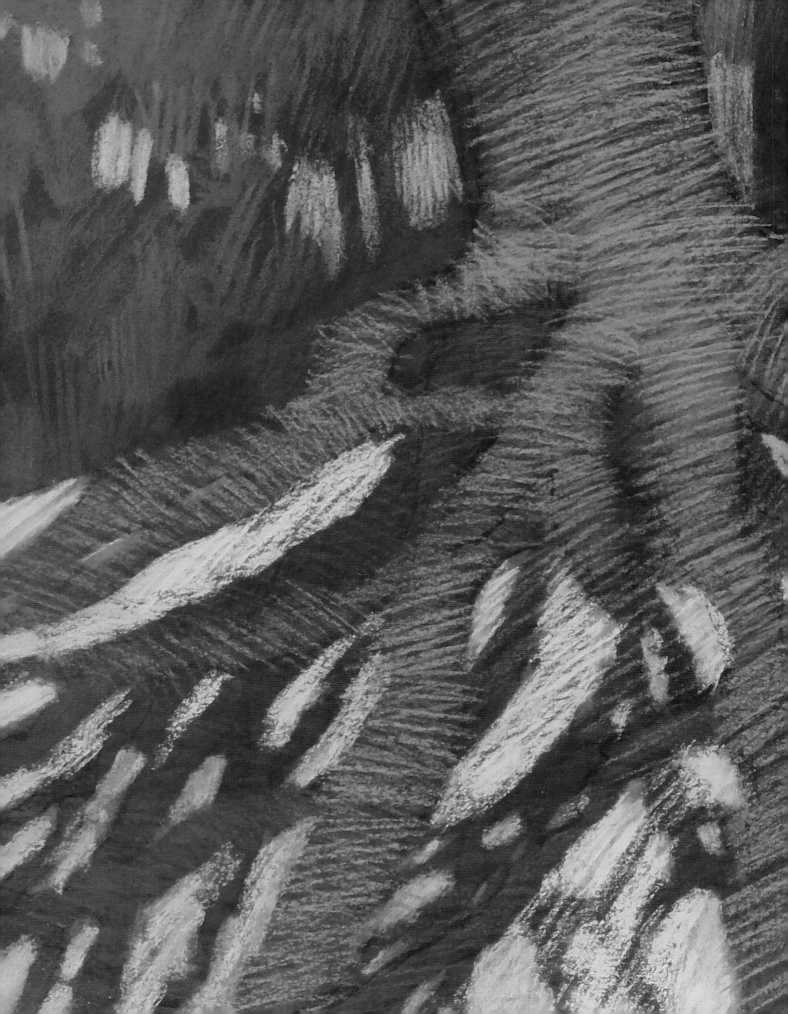

The waves have pulled away so much sand
that the tree's roots are free
and bending over the beach
with giant knees and feet.

The wind has pulled off so many needles
that the branches are free
and stretching toward the sea
with giant elbows and fingers.

A tree really can have legs
to run down the beach
and arms
to reach for the sea.

With each storm that comes,
the tree loses more needles,
and her roots become more free.
Now, when a big wind blows,
he makani Mālua,
her whispers grow so low
they almost disappear.

I sit on her knees
and dream and dream.
Together we whisper
     whaaaaaah shhhhh paaaaah
     whooooshh aaaaaaaaahhhh

     grrrrrr neckle ummmmmmmmbrrrrr

     whaaaaaah shhhhh paaaaah
     whooooshh aaaaaaaaahhhh.

About the Ironwood

The tree that stands "just on the spot where the land becomes sand" is an ironwood, a tree that comes from Australia and the warm islands of the South Pacific. Ironwoods are hardy and can survive in harsh conditions. They can grow in salty, sandy, or dry soil. They can brave bad storms and burning sunshine. For this reason, many ironwoods are planted along shorelines in places like Hawai'i, where they keep the land from washing away. Ironwood trees can grow as tall as 150 feet, so Hawaiians also use them as windbreaks along fields of papaya or coffee.

The ironwood has long, slender, drooping needles and one-inch spiky cones that look like tiny brown pineapples. Its wood is red like beef and hard like oak. In the old days, the wood was used to beat bark into tapa cloth or carved into war clubs. Today it is used for making fences.

Scientists call the tree *Casuarina equisetifolia* [cazz-you-a-reena eck-wee-settee-folee-ah]. In English it is also known as "common ironwood," "beefwood," and "she-oak," because of the sh-sh-sh sound the wind makes as it blows through the shaggy needles. The ironwood looks like a pine tree from far away, so Hawaiians named it paina [pie-nuh]. Other Polynesians call it toa [to-uh], which means "warrior tree" or "brave tree."

Legends about the Ironwood

In Fiji, legend tells of the sky child whose ironwood staff grew in one night into a tree that reached heaven. He climbed to the sky and helped his father beat his enemies, then returned to earth and married the serpent god's daughter.

Tongan legend says that only one chief dared trying to chop down the ironwood. His men spat blood the color of its inner wood, died, and were left in the tall ferns as the tree sprouted anew. Finally, Ono heard of their failure and came with his magic spade. He dug carefully, cutting the taproot in two with a mighty blow. Out popped the head of a demon. With another huge blow, he split the skull of the demon. Tongans say that groves of ironwood sprang from the chips made by Ono's spade.

Tahitians believed that ironwoods came from the bodies of fallen warriors, whose blood turned into red sap and hair into long needles. The tree's ironlike wood was carved into weapons, which were believed to possess mana, or magical powers.

In Hawai'i, the tree became a symbol of faithfulness. Japanese people who came to work in the sugar cane fields used ironwood branches as gateway decorations in their New Year's festival remembering Matsue and Teoya, whose love under the pines increased with the years. Other islanders say the ironwood has mysterious powers, and that in the shadow of the tree at full moon, secrets of the future can be heard.

Legends about Ka'ena Point

'Iwalani's ironwood tree stands on the North Shore of O'ahu in Mokulē'ia, where long white beaches stretch below lava cliffs that are carved by rains, folded by waterfalls, and softened by mosses. The beaches end at rocky Ka'ena Point, on the northwesternmost tip of the island.

Ancient Hawaiian legend says that a goddess named Ka'ena lived there. She was a cousin of the volcano goddess Pele, and her name means "red hot" or "blazing." The demigod Māui once stood on the shore of Kaua'i and cast his powerful hook toward O'ahu to unite the two islands. He managed only to loosen a huge boulder, which fell and remains to this day in the waters off Ka'ena Point.

There is another prominent boulder at Ka'ena Point, one believed to hold an important role in the cycle of life. This large limestone rock, in view of the setting sun, is known as Leina a Ka 'Uhane, or "soul's leap."* When a person dies, ancient Hawaiians believed, the soul leaves the body and wanders about the island, first going to a fishing shrine and eventually approaching the limestone rock. From there the soul leaps into Pō, the Hereafter. This is the spiritual realm where the soul joins the ancestors and lives on forever.

---

*The nineteenth-century historian Samuel Kamakau, who was born in Mokulē'ia, describes Leina a Ka 'Uhane as "a sea furrow, a leaping place into endless night."

For Teachers and Parents

'Iwalani's Tree can be used to teach children about poetry. Within the text, readers will find:

- ✓ perfect rhymes ("wood … good" or "spot … hot")
- ✓ internal rhymes ("where the land becomes sand")
- ✓ assonance ("beach … sea" and "knees … dream")
- ✓ rhythmic phrasing ("a pool of cool")
- ✓ alliteration ("branches that bend and bellow")

- ✓ onomatopoeia ("yowl," "smash," "howl," and "crack")

The book also familiarizes children with the notion of imagery ("deep dark rainforest") and simile ("lightning cracks the sky open like a coconut").

'Iwalani's Tree is sprinkled with phrases from the Hawaiian language, which is being revived in some island families. Here is a key to the pronunciation and meaning of key phrases:

* ʻIwalani (ee-vuh-lah-nee): literally, heavenly frigate bird
* he makani aheahe (hey muh-kuh-nee ah-hey-ah-hey): a light breeze
* he makani Mālua (hey muh-kuh-nee mah-loo-ah): a brisk wind

* pueo (poo-eh-oh): short-eared owl, endemic to Hawaiʻi
* puaʻa (poo-ah-ah): pig or wild boar
* moemoe (mow-eh-mow-eh): sleep

Email the author for a study guide at connie@sinandsyntax.com.

About the Author

Constance Hale has covered Hawaiian dance for the *Los Angeles Times*, sentence magic for the *New York Times*, and San Francisco politics and culture for national newspapers and magazines. Her books on language and literary style—including *Sin and Syntax* and *Vex, Hex, Smash, Smooch*—are used in classrooms across the country and the globe. She lives in California and Hawaiʻi but grew up on the beach at Mokuléʻia with many friends among the ironwood trees.

About the Illustrator

Kathleen Peterson has illustrated over twenty books. She is the founding director of the Central Utah Art Center and displays her landscape paintings in galleries around the west and on the Big Island of Hawaiʻi. A past resident of Hawaiʻi, Peterson and her husband, Steve, live on a farm in Spring City, Utah with two horses, a mule, a bunch of free-range chickens, one cat, and Pete the Dog. Her other Hawaiian children's books are: *Koa's Seed, Pele and Poliʻahu: A Tale of Fire and Ice,* and *Moon Mangoes.*

Text copyright © 2016 by Constance Hale
Illustrations copyright © 2016 by Kathleen Peterson

ISBN-10: 1-933067-80-2 / ISBN-13: 978-1-933067-80-3
Library of Congress Control Number: 2016938921
Design by Jane Gillespie
First Printing, September 2016

BeachHouse Publishing, LLC • PO Box 5464 • Kāneʻohe, Hawaiʻi 96744
info@beachhousepublishing.com
www.beachhousepublishing.com
Printed in China